CONTENTS

Jake's Wish

"I don't care if your friend Darren has a python, a cockatoo and a marmoset monkey," said Mum, "the answer's still no."

I was about to point out that I didn't actually want a pet cockatoo or marmoset monkey – a simple hamster would do – when I caught sight of Mum's hands mangling the tea-towel a bit like a boa constrictor might crush a small rodent – and I decided to keep quiet.

Mum gave the tea-towel a temporary break from mangling and shook it out instead.

"Look, Jake," she said. "We've been through all this, haven't we? Lots of times.

You know it wouldn't be right for us to take on a pet. Especially not at the moment."

I looked up with my most appealing expression – the one I usually reserve for teachers when I'm trying to get out of doing games. My eyes suddenly became the size of Frisbees.

"Yes, Mum," I said. "It's just that..."

"I know, love," Mum said, not letting me finish. "You want a pet. But it's just not possible at the moment. One day, when we've got a proper home somewhere. Then you can have a pet maybe. Umm? OK?"

What I wished for, more than anything else in the world, was a pet. I'd been trying to persuade Mum to let me have a pet for ages. But the answer was always the same. The thing was, you see, we were always moving house because of Dad's job, so I'd never had a proper home. The longest we'd lived anywhere was two years. That had been at our last place in Bristol.

I liked Bristol. But then we'd had to move again. Battersea, in south London, was where we were living now. It was only temporary, Dad said, until he found somewhere more suitable. ("Buckingham Palace is nice, I've heard," I said.) But we'd been in Battersea now for four months. Well, Mum and I had. Dad had been in Canada for the last six weeks on business. He's a trouble-shooter. I don't really know what that means, but it sounds good. It went down well at school anyway. My classmates thought Dad must be some kind of gangster – which, in Battersea, made him a bit of a hero and made settling in at school pretty easy.

I climbed down the metal fire-escape outside our back door and into the yard.

The yard was one of the best things about our new place, although really it belonged to the basement flat underneath us. Luckily, though, no one was living there at the moment, so I had the yard to myself. Mum didn't like it because it was so small and not a proper garden. It was usually full of rubbish too, like cardboard boxes and bits of string. It didn't have any flower-beds or a lawn and there was only one tree. But I didn't mind everything being small. It was sort of cosy and the area around it was interesting too.

On one side of the yard was a café or "a greasy spoon" as Mum called it. It gave off this smell of bacon and eggs and coffee all day long. But the best thing about it was that it attracted a whole lot of cats from all around the neighbourhood and, to get to the back of the café, they came through our yard. The other side, stretching right round the

back, was taken up by a scrapheap, full
of the most brilliant old cars – all rusty and
smashed-up. At that moment, a bulldozer was
crashing its way through the middle of them.

The noise was deafening. I could hardly hear myself think – and I had a lot to think about.

What I was trying to think about was Darren's dog. Darren was my best friend at school. He had several pets – a goldfish, a guinea-pig, a canary – but his favourite was Knuckles, his dog. Darren's dad wasn't so fond of Knuckles though, because he said the dog was always barking. But that's what dogs *do*, isn't it? Telling them not to bark is like telling Superman not to wear his underpants outside his trousers. Anyway, I was thinking that Darren ought to bring Knuckles round to our yard, because he could bark till he was hoarse and no one would be able to hear him.

Just as I was thinking these deep thoughts a huge, fat black tom with an enormous fluffy tail came swaggering along the wall in the direction of the café. I actually heard him before I saw him. He gave out this dreadful yowl, like a baby wailing. When he got to the end wall he yowled again. One of the workmen on the scrapheap shouted and

threw a stone at him. It skimmed over his head and landed in our yard. The tom shot along the wall and scampered down to the back of the café to join the other cats that would be gathered there.

It was my dream that one day one of those cats would jump down into our yard and come over to me and I'd stroke it and give it a saucer of milk and it would purr with pleasure. But it was only a wish, because what half-intelligent cat would pass up the chance of a string of bacon rinds for a measly saucer of milk?

It was then that I saw the cardboard box quiver.

For a few seconds I thought I was seeing things, because, as far as I was aware, cardboard boxes didn't have a life of their own – not on this planet anyway. But this box *was* moving. It quivered and then shook as though there was something trapped inside it, struggling to get out. I went over to the box and cautiously lifted one edge with a stick – just in case there was a snake or something unpleasant like that underneath. Battersea's not known for its snakes, but then, as Mum often points out, I'm not known for my logical thinking.

The box was still now and nothing came out, so I bent down, and, lifting the edge a little higher, peered in. Out of the gloom two glittering amber eyes looked back at me.

I dropped the stick and jumped back, toppling over on to the ground. When I looked up again, the box was thrashing about like a tumble-drier, and mewing. I ran over and picked up the box. A small tabby cat stood there, its back arched, its tail brush thick. I expected it to scamper away now that it had been released, but it didn't. It just stood, looking small and defensive, like a snail that had lost its shell and didn't quite know what to do next. *I* knew what to do next.

I bent down.

"Here, pussy-pussy," I sang. "Here pussy-pussy." I rubbed my fingers together and pursed my lips, making the sound that for some reason everyone makes when they're trying to attract cats. For a moment it had no effect, but then, gradually, the arch went out of the cat's back and it started to walk towards me. It rubbed against my legs and, with trembling fingers, I stroked it. Then I pinched myself to make sure I wasn't dreaming. Then I bit my lip just to make sure

the pinch I felt wasn't part of the dream.
Then I was convinced.

It was a she-cat. I think most tabby cats
are. She was lovely. She had a very intelligent
look in her eyes – very friendly too. And
when she lay down and rolled in the dust, I
saw that she had the most amazing fluffy
ginger tummy. I picked up an old piece of
string and dangled it above her face and she
swiped at it with her paw, then tried to catch
it in her teeth. When she finally succeeded,
she gripped the string and started
kicking it. It was one of the
funniest things I'd ever seen.
I knew that this was
the cat for me.

We played together like that for ages, until she got tired. Then she just flopped on her side and lay still. I thought maybe she was thirsty after all her activity. I decided that while she seemed so settled, I'd get her a saucer of milk. But I was scared that she'd leave if she saw I'd gone, so I walked very slowly and stiffly up the stairs to the kitchen, trying to make it look like I wasn't really moving at all. She didn't seem to notice me going.

The moment I was through the kitchen door I dived for the fridge and quickly filled a saucer with milk. Luckily, Mum was nowhere to be seen. I walked back out and down the fire-escape to the yard, treading carefully so as not to spill any of the milk. I'd only been away for a couple of minutes at the most. But it was long enough. I looked all around, I called and I mewed, I searched every corner of the yard – but the little tabby cat was gone.

The Cat Search

The next few days dragged terribly. Each afternoon I rushed home from school and looked out in the yard, but there was no sign of the little tabby cat. The thought crossed my mind that maybe she'd come back during the day when I hadn't been there. I considered pretending I was ill, so that I could get off school for a day. But I knew that if I managed to convince Mum that I was sick enough to miss school, then she'd make me stay in bed all day. As it was, at least I could go out in the yard when I got home in the afternoon.

Most of that week at school, Darren and I sat together during break and talked about our "pet" problems. Knuckles was in the dog-house again. One night he'd been shut in the sitting-room by mistake and when Darren's dad had found him in the morning, the dog had chewed his way right through a very big and expensive library book.

"Dad says we should never have got him," said Darren gloomily. "He says a dog like Knuckles should be in the country, not living in a flat like ours."

"Sounds just like what my mum would say," I said. Then I told him all about the little tabby cat and that seemed to cheer him up a bit.

"We had a tabby cat once," he said. "She was beautiful."

"What happened to her?" I asked. His face went all gloomy again.

"She ate some poison and died," he said. Darren didn't have much luck with his pets. He'd had runaway hamsters, rabbits eaten by foxes, and tropical fish that had eaten each other. Now he had a book-eating dog.

On Friday afternoon we finished school early and Darren came back to our flat. There was still no sign of the tabby cat, so Darren suggested we mount a local search.

We started next door in the café. I'd never been in there before and if I hadn't been with Darren I'm not sure I would have dared. The sort of people who usually went in there were what my mum called "rough types" – men and women in black leather motorcycle jackets and brawny workmen in dirty jeans, who wore T-shirts even in winter. The juke-box was playing an Elvis Presley record. Elvis Presley is one of my dad's favourites and hearing him sing made me think how much I was missing him – Dad, I mean, not Elvis. There was a delicious smell of toasted bacon sandwiches. The woman at the counter was wiping the surface with a cloth.

"Hello, duck," she said, smiling. "You're the lad from next door, aren't you? I see you coming home from school each day." She nodded at Darren. "This your friend?"

"Yes," I said.

"Well," she said, "what can I do you for?"

"I'm looking for a cat," I said timidly. "A little tabby cat."

"With a ginger tum," Darren chipped in. The woman laughed.

"There're all sorts of cats round here," she said. "More cats than customers, most of the time. Hold on a sec."

A customer had come up to the counter to pay his bill. I looked at him out of the corner of my eye. He was tall with a round red face and wore oily overalls. The woman took his money and rang up the amount on the till.

"Here, Jim," she said. "These two lads are looking for a little tabby cat with a ginger tum. That sound like one of Harry's to you?"

"Could be," said Jim. "Could be."

"Harry's the tyre man, round the corner," the woman said to us. "He's gots lots of cats."

"I'll take you there, if you like," said Jim.

"Well," I said hesitantly, not sure whether I should go off with a strange man, even if it was just round the corner.

"Don't worry," said the woman. "Jim won't eat you. Not after what he's just tucked away in here."

Jim laughed. "I'm going to see Harry anyway," he said. "So, you can follow me if you want."

"See you, Cheryl," he added. Then he walked out.

Darren and I looked at each other.

"Come on!" he said and we ran out of the café.

Harry's place was a big garage stacked full of tyres. Harry looked like he was full of tyres too. His huge stomach was bursting out of the blue boiler suit he was wearing.

"I hear you're looking for a moggy," he said, fingering his small moustache. Darren and I both nodded.

"A little tabby cat which my friend saw in his back yard," said Darren. "We wondered if she might be yours."

"Ah," said Harry, rubbing his moustache some more. "Well, she could be. I've got cats coming out of my ears in here, you know. Keeps the vermin away."

"Mice and rats," Jim explained. "We get a lot round here, being as how we're so near the river." Darren started to look very interested.

"I've never had a rat," he said. "I had a pet mouse once though."

"Nasty things, rats," said Harry. "Gnaw their way right through a tyre they will, give them half a chance. They'd ruin my stock they would, if I didn't have the cats to keep them at bay."

As if on cue, a big white cat with a black patch over his eye and a stumpy tail darted from behind a pile of tyres and out of the garage.

"Going for his supper round at the café, no doubt," said Harry. He picked up a tool and started levering the rim of a tyre. "Well, I must get on."

Darren and I shuffled in the doorway.

Jim saw us and nodded.

"What about that tabby cat, Harry?" he asked. "Is he one of yours or what?"

Harry carried on working. "Yeah," he said.

"Sounds like it."

I looked around the garage with new interest, hoping against hope that I might see the little tabby cat. But I couldn't.

"Has she got a name?" I asked. Harry waved his tool in the air.

"Name!" he cried. "My mogs don't have names. They're alley-cats. You won't find no Tiddles or Fluffy round here."

"Names," he said again and shook his head.

"At least you know she's definitely around here somewhere," said Darren, as we walked back towards the flat.

"Yeah," I said, but without much enthusiasm. To tell the truth, I was a bit disappointed to find out that my tabby cat belonged to someone else. I suppose I'd been hoping that we'd find out she was a stray – not that there was a hope of her being my cat anyway, with the way Mum felt on the subject of pets. But at least I could have pretended she was mine.

Miss Barnes Moves In

When we came back round the corner I saw that there was a small white van parked outside our flat and Mum was standing on the street talking to an old lady. She caught sight of us as we came past the café and waved.

"Ah, there you are," she said. "Just in time."

"In time for what?" I asked.

"To help with Miss Barnes' things." Mum turned towards the old lady.

"Miss Barnes is moving in downstairs," she said. The old lady was looking at me and smiling. It was a very friendly, nice smile – the

sort of catchy smile that makes you smile too,
but without knowing that you are.

"You must be Jake," she said.

"Yes," I said. "And this is Darren."

"I hope you don't mind helping me," Miss
Barnes said. "I haven't a great deal. Just a few
little trinkets. My nephew Paul will unload
the heavy objects."

A young man wearing glasses appeared from behind the van, struggling with a suitcase that was almost as big as he was.

"Hi," he said cheerfully, as he staggered past us down the stairs to the basement flat.

"Come on," I said to Darren and we went round the back of the van to see what we could carry.

"I'll put the kettle on," said Mum.

Miss Barnes didn't bring any furniture with her, because the basement flat was already furnished. It was mainly plants and rectangular-shaped parcels which felt like pictures that Darren and I carried in, while Paul managed all the bags and boxes. There weren't all that many, but by the time the van was empty his face was bright red and he looked completely exhausted.

"You look like you could do with a drink," Mum said, carrying in a tray of tea and orange juice. Paul nodded, but was too out of breath to reply.

"I'm sure I have some cake here

somewhere," said Miss Barnes. "Now, where did I put it?" For a moment, she stood frowning at the mass of parcels, bags, boxes and plants. Then she went over to the huge suitcase that Paul had carried in.

"In here, I think," she said. After a bit of rummaging, she pulled out a tin.

"Eureka!" she cried, with one of those special smiles which made all of us smile too. "We have cake."

The cake turned out to be a sponge with lots of raspberry jam in the middle. It was delicious. Darren and I had two and a half slices each. Paul had three – in about as many minutes – then said he had to go.

"I've got a lecture at five," he said.

"Paul's studying architecture," Miss Barnes said to Mum. "He works very hard." Paul went as red as the raspberry jam he'd just eaten.

"Well, thanks very much for helping, dear," Miss Barnes said to him. "Do come and visit me soon, won't you?"

She opened her purse, took out a ten pound note and pressed it into his hand. "A little token of my appreciation," she said. Then she stuck her head forward a little for him to give her a goodbye kiss.

After Paul had gone, Mum and Miss Barnes talked for a little about their families and other things. Miss Barnes said she'd just come back from a cruise to Australia.

"I try to go somewhere warm most winters," she said. "It's good for my rusty old joints." Mum told Miss Barnes about Dad being in Canada.

"Which reminds me," she said, "he said he'd call about now, so I'd better get back."

She looked at Darren and me. "Come on, you two."

"Oh, Mum," I moaned, not wanting to go yet.

Miss Barnes smiled. "They can stay for a while, if they like," she said. "We can do some sorting together."

"Yes, please," I said. I had a feeling that we might find some interesting things in all those parcels.

"OK, then," Mum agreed. "No more cake, though," she said to me. "You'll be having your tea in half an hour."

Miss Barnes went over to one of the boxes which was packed with lots of newspaper.

"Now, let's see what treasures we have in here," she said and pulled something out.

"It's like a 'Lucky Dip', isn't it?" she said. "Who knows what we might find."

What she found wasn't treasure though, it was a china cup. She must have seen the disappointment on our faces, because she pulled a funny expression and said, "Mmmm, not really very interesting, is it? Unless you're an old fuddy-duddy like me. Perhaps you'll have more luck, Jake."

I put my hand in the box, but I didn't take any of the things on the top, in case they were just cups too. I delved right down and pulled out something very small and square, definitely not a tea cup. I took the newspaper off and uncovered a little brightly painted box. I opened it up, but there was nothing inside.

"I've had that for years and years," said Miss Barnes. "My father brought it back from China."

"Have you ever been to China?" Darren asked.

"No," she said, "I never have." She shook her head and looked a little sad for a moment. Then she perked up again and said, "Let's see what you can find, Darren."

Darren put his hand down inside the box and pulled out a package, larger than the one I'd found. He took off a layer of newspaper, then another, then another.

"It's like 'pass the parcel'," he said, peeling off the last piece of wrapping. The object wasn't much bigger than the Chinese box, but much heavier. It was a green cat, very slim and sleek with deep-set black eyes and tall, pointy ears. I'd never seen a cat like it before.

"Ah, Cleopatra," sighed Miss Barnes, "my Egyptian cat. Isn't she splendid? Made of copper, I think. They're two a penny in Cairo, of course, but you don't see many in this country."

"It's great," I said.

"Terrific," agreed Darren.

"She's one of my very favourite things,"

said Miss Barnes. "I brought her back with me from Egypt many years ago. There's a legend attached to her – well, so the man said who sold her to me. Although I expect he spins the same yarn to every tourist. But there is something rather magical about her, don't you think?"

"Yes," I said. She was certainly having a magical effect on me – I couldn't take my eyes off her.

"Would you like to hear an Egyptian joke?" Darren asked.

"Yes indeed I would," said Miss Barnes enthusiastically. (She hadn't ever heard one of Darren's jokes before.)

"Where can you find an old Pharaoh in London?" said Darren. Miss Barnes concentrated hard. "That's a difficult one," she said. "I really don't know. The British Museum perhaps."

"No," said Darren. "Tooting Common." Miss Barnes looked puzzled for a moment. Then she smiled.

"Tooting Common," she said. "Very good. Tutankhamun, Tooting Common."

"Tutankhamun was a Pharaoh," Darren explained.

"I can see you know your Egyptology," said Miss Barnes, which shut Darren up for a minute and gave me the chance to ask about the green cat.

"Will you tell us the legend about Cleopatra?" I asked. But before Miss Barnes could reply, Darren interrupted again.

"Jake's got a cat," he said. "Well, sort of."

"She belongs to the tyre man round the corner," I said. "I've only seen her once." I told Miss Barnes about the little tabby cat and what Mum had said about me not having pets.

"Yes, well, I see your mother's point," said Miss Barnes. "I'm sure you'll settle somewhere soon. It's only old sea dogs like me who spend their lives on the move. My father was a sea captain, you see, so travelling's in my blood."

Just as Miss Barnes finished speaking, I
caught sight of something outside in the yard.
I jumped up and ran over to the french
windows.

"Look!" I cried. "She's back!" The little
tabby cat was sitting by the window,
miaowing.

"Ah, the prodigal returns," said Miss Barnes. Together Darren and I unbolted the windows and the cat came trotting in. She rubbed herself against my legs like she had the first time. Then she did the same to Miss Barnes.

"What a lovely cat, Jake," Miss Barnes said. "Why don't you pour her a saucer of milk?"

My hand was shaking when I poured the milk I was so excited. The three of us sat in silence, grinning as we watched the cat drink her milk. Then Darren crumpled some of the newspaper wrapping into a ball to throw for her.

"I'll show you a game she really likes," I said. I went outside to get a piece of string – and she followed me. I was just dangling the string in front of her nose when Mum appeared at the top of the fire-escape.

"Time for dinner, Jake," she said. Then she saw the cat.

"Jake," she said. "You know I don't want you encouraging these stray cats. It won't be fair to them when we move away."

Suddenly, my heart dropped to the soles of my feet and I couldn't think of anything to say. Miss Barnes could, though.

"It's all right, Mrs Gorman," she said. "It's not a stray – she's my cat." She looked at me with one of her catching smiles. "Thank you very much for helping me, Jake, and you too, Darren. Now, off you both go for your supper."

"Thanks, Miss Barnes," I said happily and I gave her a big smile. I knew I'd got myself a very special new friend.

Canada

That evening my head was so full of the tabby cat and the arrival of Miss Barnes that I found it hard to sleep. But when I did I had the most brilliant dream about being in Egypt with the green cat and an old lady who looked a bit like Miss Barnes and a bit like my grandma, who lives in Australia. I don't know why I dreamed about Grandma because I haven't seen her for ages, but it was really great seeing her again – even if it *was* only in a dream.

When I came down to breakfast I was feeling sunnier than the bowl of Golden Frosties Mum had put on the table for me.

But she'd got a nasty shock for me.

"Jake," said Mum, "your dad phoned last night after you'd gone to bed. He's been offered a permanent job in Canada. A very good job and a house as well – in Toronto. He says it's lovely there. He'd like to accept, but he wants to know how you feel about it first. There's no rush. We can decide when Dad comes home, but I want you to think about it carefully. OK?"

My mood suddenly experienced a major weather change – from sunny to heavily overcast. It must have been very obvious because Mum said, "Your dad says it's very nice over in Canada, Jake, and we'd have a settled home. But it's not definite. It's just an idea."

I was too shocked to say anything. I just stared at my cereal. *Canada*, I thought. *Canada*. I didn't want to go anywhere – and certainly not to Canada. Canada was on the other side of the world. Suddenly I felt like I was going to cry, so I got up from the table and stumbled outside. I climbed down to the yard, kicking the steps of the fire-escape as I went – clang, clang, clang – till I got to the bottom. Then I sat on the last step, put my chin in my hand and scowled.

I was so deep in my misery that I didn't notice the little tabby cat until she brushed against my leg and started to miaow. I looked down and there she was, gazing up at me with her big lime-green eyes.

"Hello, puss," I said sadly, and I scratched her head gently. She started to purr. Then a moment later, she was lying under the bottom step with her ginger tummy in the air and I had to smile because she looked so funny, rolling from side to side, kicking her legs in the air.

I heard a knocking on glass and looked round to see Miss Barnes standing at her french windows. She waved and then pointed at a saucer of milk she was holding. I nodded

and waved back. She opened her french windows and came out slowly into the yard. I noticed that she had quite a big limp and she had trouble holding the saucer steady, so I jumped up and ran over to take it from her.

"There you go," she said, giving it to me.

I put it down on the ground and the cat came over and sniffed at it. Then she started to lap the milk with her tiny tongue.

Miss Barnes hobbled towards me.

"Are you all right?" I asked.

"Ooh," she said. "It's just my old bones. They always play up in the morning. You wouldn't be a very kind boy and fetch my stick, would you, Jake? I left it by the window."

I went in and brought out the stick.

"Perhaps we should tempt her inside," said Miss Barnes. "Get her used to coming in. Once she realizes there's a nice, cosy, warm place waiting for her whenever she wants it, she'll be hooked. Until she finds somewhere better, of course. Cats are like that."

"My cat's special," I said proudly, gazing at the little cat, who was now delicately licking her paws.

"She is," said Miss Barnes, "she really is."

Miss Barnes had done quite a lot more unpacking since the afternoon before. The first thing I noticed was the green cat, Cleopatra, standing on the mantelpiece. She looked very royal, like she owned the flat. All round her, Miss Barnes had propped up pictures of the sea and ships.

"You must like the sea a lot," I said.

"Ah, yes," Miss Barnes sighed. "Yes, indeed. It's my one true love."

"Why don't you live by the sea then?" I asked. I thought that sounded a bit rude, so I added: "What I mean is, it's a long way from the sea here."

"It is, isn't it?" Miss Barnes agreed. "But you see, Jake, I've lived by the sea most of my life – now I'm old and rickety like an ancient ship and I need to live near people who can look after me should I start sinking. My sister and brother-in-law live round here, and my nephew Paul, whom you met yesterday. He has promised, very kindly, to take me on an outing to Brighton, during his next holidays."

"That's good," I said.

"Yes," she said. She looked across to where the little tabby cat was getting herself comfortable in an armchair.

"Puss seems to be making herself at home all right," she said. I smiled.

"Ah, that's better," she said. "When I saw you sitting out there on the steps with an expression like rolling thunder, I was quite concerned. Whatever can be the matter with Jake? I asked myself. He seemed such a cheerful soul when I met him yesterday. I hope he's not angry because he's got to share his yard with a funny old lady."

"Oh no," I said. "It's not that. I'm glad you've moved in. Honest. It's something else." I told her about Dad's phone call and my conversation with Mum.

"Have you been to Canada?" I asked.

"I have," said Miss Barnes. "A long time ago. It's very pleasant. The people are very friendly – and it's very, very big. Bigger than the United States – though there are fewer people, of course."

"I don't like big places," I said. "I want to stay here with you and Puss and Cleopatra. I like it here."

"Well," said Miss Barnes. "You are still very young, Jake, and there are lots of things for you to experience. Lots of very wonderful things too. The world is your oyster. If I were your age now, I would leap at the opportunity of going to Canada." I looked at Miss Barnes with a frown.

"Don't you want me to stay?" I said, because I thought she'd have been on my side – not Mum's.

"Naturally," she said. "But that would be selfish. What I really want is what is best for you, Jake. I'm sure your mother and father do too." I didn't say anything.

"Have you told your mother what you feel about going to Canada?" Miss Barnes asked. I stared at my shoes. "No," I said miserably.

"Well, you must, Jake. You must tell her just what you've told me."

I tried for a moment to imagine having this same conversation with Mum. But I couldn't. It would be like when I asked her about having a pet. She wouldn't really listen to me.

The little tabby cat was curled up in the armchair now with her eyes closed. I sat down by her and stroked her head.

"I couldn't leave my Puss," I said.

"Ah," said Miss Barnes. "Cats are great roamers too, you know. You can never really own a cat. They own you for a while – and if you're lucky, they stay put. But it's not really in their instincts. Look at Cleopatra there. She has travelled with me all over the world, but there's something in her eyes that always seems to be elsewhere. I often think, when I look at her, that if she were made of flesh and blood rather than copper, she would have gone away years ago. Not because she doesn't like me, but because it's in a cat's nature to be on the move."

"I don't think Puss is going to move for a while," I said. "She's lovely and cosy."

I put my face against the soft, warm fur of her back and wished that she would stay with me for ever.

Rats!

The next week was a pretty good one. Mum didn't mention Canada once and I started to hope that maybe she and Dad had decided not to go and live there after all. Darren said that if I went to Canada he'd look after my cat, which was another reason why I hoped the whole thing would fall through. He was looking for another pet, he said, because his dad had finally decided Knuckles had to go after the dog had jumped straight through their glass front door trying to get at the milkman.

I went down to Miss Barnes' flat every day – for a few minutes in the morning before going to school and then for about an hour when I got home. Puss was usually there, but if she wasn't, then all I had to do was go out in the yard and call "Puss, Puss" and in she'd come. Then we'd have a great time playing together. Miss Barnes even bought some tins of cat food so that I could feed Puss. The only problem was that Mum was beginning to get suspicious. She said I was spending too much time down at Miss Barnes' and that I was getting too attached to her cat.

"Sometimes," she said, "I wonder who that cat really belongs to."

"I'm just helping Miss Barnes look after her," I said.

"Her," said Mum. "Well, I hope she's been done. Otherwise we'll have a whole lot of kittens around the place and no doubt you'll be pestering me for one."

Kittens! I thought – and it was a very exciting thought indeed. I hoped like anything that Puss hadn't been "done" – whatever that meant – although I had no idea how you could tell. I could have gone and asked Harry the tyre man, I suppose, but then he might have been annoyed that I'd taken his cat away.

The week passed quickly and soon it was Friday afternoon again. I invited Darren to come round and see Puss, because I thought it might stop him thinking about Knuckles, who was off to his new owner in the country the next day. But just as we were about to go down to Miss Barnes' flat, Mum stopped us.

"I want a word with you, Jake," she said.

"Oh, hi Mum," I said. "I thought you were out."

"I was," she said. "I just popped over to the shops to get something for your tea. And I ran into the woman from the café next door."

"Oh yes," I said, trying to sound casual, but feeling a bit nervous.

"Yes," she said. "And do you know what she said to me?" I shook my head.

"She asked if you'd found your cat yet. 'What cat is that?' I asked her. 'A little tabby one,' she said. 'Your lad came into the café last week asking if anyone had seen it.'"

Mum looked at me with an expression which suggested that at any moment she was going to give me some of that mangling treatment she usually reserved for tea-towels.

"Well?" she said. "And don't say it's Miss Barnes' cat, because Miss Barnes hadn't moved in when you went out on your search."

I shuffled my feet uncomfortably and so did Darren. I frowned and tried to make up an explanation that would fool Mum. But it was too late. I looked up and was just about to try and explain that it hadn't been Miss Barnes' cat then but it *was* her cat now, in a manner of speaking, when Mum's face suddenly went as white as milk and her eyes as wide as saucers. She put her hand to her mouth.

"Oh my God!" she cried. "Oh no!"

Darren and I turned around to see what Mum was looking at. At the top of the fire-escape, sniffing around by the back door was a small grey rat. I thought it was a mouse at first – until I saw its long, spindly tail.

"Wow!" said Darren. "A rat," and he started to go towards the back door.

"Don't go near it, Darren!" Mum cried. "And don't open the door. Rats are nasty and very vicious. They've got very sharp teeth."

Darren peered out through the glass. "I think he looks rather nice," he said. "He's probably just hungry."

I went and stood beside Darren. Seeing the rat close up made me shiver.

"Rats have to bite things all the time," said Darren, "because their teeth are always growing. If they didn't bite, then their teeth would grow so big they wouldn't be able to fit in their mouths."

"Thank you, Darren," Mum said, without sounding very grateful. Then she gasped as two little grey heads popped up over the fence which backed on to the scrapyard. In a flurry of fur and tail they scuttled down into our yard and inside a hole in the café's wall.

"They must be going to the café to look

for food," Darren said.

"They won't last long round there," I said. "Not with all those cats."

"Thank God for those cats," Mum said, which was a bit of a turnabout, I thought, considering what she'd just been saying. "Where's that cat of yours, Jake? We could do with him now."

"Her," I said automatically. Darren shook his head. "You need poison," he said, matter-of-factly. "Rats attack cats. They can give them a very nasty bite. One of our cats had to go to the vet for an operation after a rat bit her. She..."

Mum interrupted: "Thank you, Darren, we don't really want to hear the gory details. Do something useful and bang on the window, will you? Perhaps that'll scare it off."

It was my turn now to go white with fear – not for myself, but for my cat. What if a rat got her? She might turn up at any moment and get into a fight with this rat on our fire-escape or the others in the scrapyard. How many rats were there? There might be hundreds, thousands. And she was such a little cat, she wouldn't stand a chance. I found myself starting to sweat, hoping for the first time that she wouldn't show up; hoping that she'd be round at Harry's or snuggled up in Miss Barnes' armchair. If she was there, then she'd be safe – at least for the moment. I needed to find out if she was or not.

Darren was banging on the window and shouting "Shoo!" but the rat didn't seem to be taking any notice at all. It just stood quite still, raising its head now and then, and twitching its whiskers. Meanwhile, another rat appeared, scampering over the fence into our yard.

"Right," said Mum. "I'm going to make a phone call. Whatever you do, don't open that door, and don't go outside."

"If I had a box, I could catch that rat," Darren said when Mum had gone. "I've got an old hamster cage at home that I could put it in. Rats make good pets I should think.

They're very intelligent. I saw a woman on the Tube carrying one on her shoulder once."

"Never mind about your rats," I said, hopping about from foot to foot. "I'm worried about my Puss. I've got to find out where she is. She might be lying wounded somewhere. She might be..." But I didn't want to think about what might be happening to Puss. I just wanted to find her and make sure she was all right.

"I've got to go down to see if she's in Miss Barnes' flat," I said, getting panicky now. I thought Darren would object, but he didn't.

"OK," he said. "I'll deal with the rat, while you go down." Carefully, like he was moving in slow motion, he opened the back door and slipped out, waving to me to follow. I could see he was having a great time. He looked like he was pretending to be an Indian brave sneaking up on a sleeping cowboy. The rat didn't move. Quietly I crept down the stairs and knocked on Miss Barnes' back door.

Puss was lying in her favourite place on the

armchair. She rolled over and stretched lazily when I called her name.

"Oh, Puss," I said, feeling incredibly relieved, "thank goodness you're here." I went over and gave her a big hug. I told Miss Barnes about the rats. She said she was sure my cat would be able to look after herself, but if it would make me happier she'd get some cat litter and keep her in for a while – until something had been done about the rats.

"They are the most amazing creatures, rats," she said. "They get everywhere. Even on board ships. What we need is a Pied Piper."

Miss Barnes came back with me to talk to Mum. Both Darren and the rat had vanished from the fire-escape. Mum gave me a cross look when I went in.

"I thought I told you not to open the door and not to go out," she said.

"He was worried about my cat," said Miss Barnes. Mum looked at her the way she looks at me sometimes when she thinks I'm not telling the truth. Miss Barnes pulled a face. "He was worried about *our* cat," she said.

"Yes, I know all about that," said Mum. But she didn't sound angry.

"I think I need a cup of tea," she said.

"What an excellent idea," Miss Barnes agreed. "You sit down and I'll put the kettle on." The one thing grown-ups always seem to agree on is the need for tea.

"Where's Darren?" I asked.

"He scuttled off home," said Mum, "clutching an old shoe box."

"Oh dear," I said. Mum turned in the doorway and sighed.

"What now?" she said.

"Oh, nothing," I lied. "I was just thinking about the rat problem."

"The Council are sending someone first thing tomorrow morning," said Mum. "If we're still here then."

"You sit down and put your feet up, dear," said Miss Barnes. "Jake and I will bring the tea through. And don't worry – we will soon have everything shipshape and Bristol fashion." Then she gave Mum and me the biggest, loveliest smile and I thought things might just turn out OK yet.

Cleopatra

Mum wouldn't go near the back of the flat
that evening. She sent me out to the kitchen if
she wanted anything and Miss Barnes and I
made the tea. We made banana and honey,
and cheese and pickle sandwiches. It was
great. Best of all though, Mum asked me to
bring Puss upstairs for the night. She said
she'd feel safer having a cat around, even
though there was no way any of the rats
could get inside. Not that they didn't try. I
didn't tell Mum, but one time when I went
out to the kitchen there was a rat climbing up
the window. As I watched, it slid down, paws
spread out, and fell on to the fire-escape

again. It was sort of funny and creepy at the same time.

Miss Barnes stayed for most of the evening and we played cards and watched TV. Puss made herself comfortable as usual. She even jumped up on to Mum's lap for a while and Mum smiled and stroked her.

"She's lovely, isn't she, Mum?" I said.

"I suppose she is quite sweet," Mum said. "Miss Barnes is very lucky." I knew from the way she looked at me that she meant that Puss's stay in our flat was only temporary – but at least she likes her, I thought.

Later in the evening, Darren rang and said the rat he'd taken home had gnawed its way through the cardboard box and escaped. He wanted to come round the next day and catch another one. Then there was a lot of noise on the other end of the line and I heard his mum say, "Darren, you are not bringing a rat into this house. Do I make myself clear?"

"Sorry, Jake," Darren said. "I'd better go now." I told Mum.

"There's something not quite right about that boy," she said, shaking her head.

That night, Puss came and slept with me. She walked around on the bed for a bit, purring, then she burrowed her way underneath the bed-cover, until all I could see of her was a lump. It would have been the happiest night of my life – except that I couldn't help thinking about Canada and how I didn't want to go. Somehow, I had to get Mum and Dad to agree with me. Miss Barnes had been right – I'd have to say something.

The rat man came about nine o'clock the next morning. He was very large. He had big black boots and a big black bag. His moustache and eyebrows were big and black too.

"Right," he said. "Let's go and have a look at the problem, shall we?" He went outside and I followed him.

"You be careful, Jake," Mum said. But there wasn't a rat to be seen. Miss Barnes opened her french windows.

"Good morning, all," she said. She looked at the rat man.

"You must be the Pied Piper," she said. "I hope you've got a magic flute in that bag of yours."

The rat man shook his head. "We do it a little more scientifically these days, madam," he said. "Now, where are the little blighters?"

"They come from over in the scrapyard," I said, pointing to our back fence. The rat man nodded. He went to the fence and peered over.

"Ah," he said, after a few minutes.

"Mmmm. I see."

He strode back to the bottom of the fire-escape where his bag was and stroked his big black moustache.

"They're clearing the scrapyard to build on," he said, "and in doing so, they've disturbed the rats who were living there. They've opened up the drains too, which hasn't helped matters." He bent down and rooted around in his bag.

"What we have," he said, "is a colony of homeless rats."

"A colony," Miss Barnes repeated.

"Just a small one probably," the rat man said reassuringly.

"What's a colony?" I asked.

"It's a sort of group or community," Miss Barnes explained. The rat man pulled a pair of big black gloves out of his bag. "Right," he said. "Time to get busy."

For the next half an hour or so, the rat man wandered round our yard, prodding here and there with a stick and muttering. He said he

was looking for the best places to put the poison.

"Is the poison dangerous for cats too?" I asked, worried about Puss.

"Well," he said, "it certainly won't do them any good, that's for sure. That's one of the reasons I need to find the right spot to put this stuff. Places like this." He opened the door of a cupboard outside Miss Barnes' flat.

"See that," he said, pointing inside. "Droppings. That's the boiler in there you see – very attractive for a rat, a boiler is. Nice and warm and cosy. So that's the first place we'll put the poison. I don't think any cat's going to go in there, do you?" I shook my head. Then I saw Puss standing at the kitchen window and I went inside to feed her.

Darren came round in the afternoon and I told him about the rat man's visit.

"You should've phoned me," he complained. "I'd love to have seen him at work. I might have picked up some useful tips."

"Useful for what?" I said.

"I don't know," he shrugged. "Just useful."
I could see he wasn't really feeling himself
and I knew why. Knuckles had gone that
morning. Darren and his dad had taken him
to his new owner in the country.

"It's a nice place," Darren said. "It's a sort
of farm and there's lots of space for Knuckles
to go walking. There're other dogs there too.
Dad says he'll be much happier." He looked
down and I knew that it was because there
were tears in his eyes. "He knew we were
leaving him," he said. "When I said goodbye
and kissed him on the nose, his tail drooped
really low and he looked all sad." Two long
tears ran down his cheeks.

"Don't worry, Darren," I said. "At least he's gone to a good home. He'll probably have a great time. You can help me look after Puss, if you like. We can share her."

"You'll be going soon too, though," Darren said gloomily.

"Not if I can help it," I said, sounding more optimistic than I actually felt.

"Let's go and see Miss Barnes," I suggested. "She's got some great pictures. We could ask her to tell us that story about the green cat."

Miss Barnes said she'd be delighted to tell us Cleopatra's story.

"It's a very ancient tale," she said. "More ancient even than I am." She smiled and so did we. Darren said later that he thought Miss Barnes must be at least a hundred.

"Cleopatra lived in about 500 BC in Ancient Egypt," Miss Barnes began. She looked up at the green cat. "Isn't that right, Your Highness?" she said. I looked at the green cat on the mantelpiece. The way she was sitting, straight up with her tall ears stiff, as though she were listening to us, she really did look like a queen.

"The Ancient Egyptians were the first people to keep cats as pets," Miss Barnes went on, "and Cleopatra was one of many who lived at the court of the Pharaoh. In those days, cats were sacred. They were thought to be the favourite creatures of Bastet, the daughter of the great sun god Re, and to have magical powers. They were considered to be very lucky and anyone who harmed one could be sentenced to death."

Cleopatra, Miss Barnes told us, didn't really belong to any one person in particular, although she was pretty keen on a boy called Ra, who often brought her a bowl of milk when she was thirsty. Ra was the only son of the Pharaoh and should have taken over when the old ruler died. But Ra's wicked uncle wanted to be Pharaoh and so he seized the throne, claiming Ra was an impostor who was really only the son of one of the royal serving women. He had Ra thrown into the palace dungeon – much to the sadness of Cleopatra. The people were unhappy, too, because most of them liked Ra and thought he was the true Pharaoh. So the wicked uncle set a test, which he reckoned would turn the people against Ra. He put three boxes on the floor of the palace hall. Under one, he placed an image of the sun god, saying that if Ra were the true Pharaoh, he would have no difficulty finding it, because Pharaohs were supposed to be gods as well. But the uncle was a magician and he tricked the people by making the image disappear, so that there was nothing at all under any of the boxes. Only one pair of eyes saw this trick – Cleopatra's. She swished her tail angrily, but what could she, a mere cat, do?

Ra was brought into the room, Miss Barnes said, and made to sit down before the boxes. Then the test was put to him. He thought and he thought, and the more he thought the deeper his frown got, because he knew that he wasn't a god. He was just a boy like Darren and me, and all he could do was guess and hope he was lucky. Just as he was about to make his choice, though, Cleopatra leapt out from where she'd been sitting and ran at the boxes, knocking over each of them in turn with her paw. Now the people could see they had been tricked and they were very angry. They seized the uncle and threw him into the palace dungeon. Ra was made Pharaoh and ruled for many years. Cleopatra lived with him and was treated like a star. People thought she brought good luck and lots of pictures and statues were made of her – like the one Miss Barnes had on her mantelpiece.

"You might also be interested to know, Jake, while we're on the subject of Ancient Egypt," Miss Barnes went on, "that another name for the goddess Bastet is Pasht, which is where we get our word 'Puss' from."

Up until then I'd been calling my cat "Puss" because I hadn't been able to think of anything better. Hearing now that it had connections with Ancient Egypt made it seem a bit less ordinary, but it still didn't seem like much of a name for such a special cat. She should have a name like Cleopatra. I looked up at the beautiful green Egyptian cat and for an instant I imagined she was alive, like the cat in the story, and had magical powers. Perhaps she could bring me good luck, I thought. I stared at her and wondered. Then I made a wish.

"Oh, Cleopatra," I said to myself, "please make Mum and Dad decide not to go to Canada. Please make them live here."

I looked into the green cat's dark eyes – but I couldn't see any sign that she had heard me.

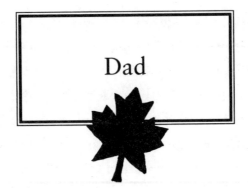

Dad

When I opened my eyes on Sunday morning, I got a real surprise.

"Dad!" I said. He was sitting on the edge of my bed, smiling. His face was very tanned. He kissed me on the forehead.

"Hiya, chuck," he said. "I see you've got yourself a new sleeping companion." He nodded towards the bottom of the bed where Puss's head was just peeping out from under the covers.

"That's Puss," I said.

"I know," he said. "I've heard all about Puss and the rats and our new neighbour. It sounds as though you've been having quite a time while I've been away."

He handed me a package wrapped in red paper and tied with gold ribbon.

"Here's a little something from Canada," he said. When I saw the package my heart leapt with excitement, but the moment Dad mentioned Canada the excitement dropped a little.

I unwrapped the package slowly. Inside was a sports shirt. It was white with a black 7 on both sides and a red leaf on the front. It looked like an American football shirt.

"Thanks, Dad," I said.

"It's a Canadian ice hockey shirt," Dad explained. "The maple leaf is the Canadian emblem."

"Oh," I said, trying to sound more enthusiastic than I was. The shirt was great and it was wonderful to see Dad, but at that moment the only thing I wanted to hear about Canada was that we weren't going to move there.

After breakfast, I took Dad downstairs to meet Miss Barnes. Just by the bottom step there was a small rat. Dad almost trod on it, but it didn't move. Dad bent down and then pushed it with his foot. It stayed still.

"It's dead," Dad said. "That poison must be doing its job." I felt a bit sorry for the little rat.

"It's only a baby," I said.

"Yes," said Dad. "But baby rats soon grow into big rats, you know. And then, before you know it, they have babies themselves."

"I suppose so," I said.

Dad and Miss Barnes got on really well. They talked for ages about all the places they'd been. Between them I think they'd gone just about everywhere in the whole world. They chatted for a while about Canada too. I was hoping Dad might say what a terrible place it was – or how much nicer England was. But he didn't. He talked about how friendly the people were, how much cleaner everything was, the lovely lake and countryside... In the end I left them to it and went upstairs to see Puss. Mum said she'd been scratching at the windows and miaowing to be let out. I got a piece of string to try and distract her.

Dad went to bed after lunch and I helped Mum with the washing up. I thought that might give her the chance to talk about Canada again, so I could tell her just how I felt. I reckoned it would be better to tackle Mum and Dad separately. But she didn't say anything about it. I'd just plucked up the courage to mention the subject myself, when she ruffled my hair and said she was feeling tired and was going up to bed for a while too. I didn't want to be on my own so I phoned Darren and he said he'd come round.

"It's too quiet here now that Knuckles has gone," he grumbled.

While Mum and Dad slept, Darren and I sat out at the top of the fire-escape, drowning our sorrows in a can of Coke. I held Puss on my lap and stroked her, but soon she started to struggle.

"I think she wants to go off. Cats don't like being cooped up too long," Darren said. "She probably misses her friends round at the café."

"I can't let you go, Puss," I said. "There're nasty rats around, and poison too. You're only a small cat and you might get hurt." Puss didn't seem to think much of my worries though. She struggled even harder and dug her claws into my arm.

"She'll be all right," said Darren. "She's an alley-cat. Besides, she's not all that small now. Look at her." I lifted Puss up a little and inspected her. Darren was right, she was definitely fatter. It must have been all the Whiskas she was eating.

Puss didn't like being held in the air. She wriggled and kicked. Then she hissed fiercely and nipped my arm with her teeth. The bite took me by surprise and I let go of her. She ran down the fire-escape, past where the dead rat had been, up on to the café wall and then leapt down out of sight.

"Puss!" I called, but she'd gone.

"I hope she'll be all right," I said.

"We might see her catch a few rats, if we sit here for a bit," said Darren, who seemed to have forgotten that only the day before he'd wanted a rat as a pet.

"Or a rat might catch her," I said gloomily. We sat for a while in silence, like a couple of statues. Then Darren said, "I wonder what Knuckles is doing now."

"I bet he's having a better time than us," I said.

"Yeah," Darren agreed. "I wouldn't mind living in the country. All those animals..."

While Darren day-dreamed about life in the country, my thoughts turned to Canada again. I just couldn't imagine what it would be like, living in a foreign country, going to a foreign school, playing strange games... But if Mum and Dad had decided to go, then what could I say to make them change their minds? They weren't going to take any notice of me. Maybe I should start trying to get used to the idea – try and find out a bit more about the place.

There were lots of old geography books in the school library and there was bound to be one on Canada. Miss Barnes might even have one. But the thing was, I didn't want to go. I didn't want to leave Puss and Miss Barnes and Darren and all my other friends at school. I was happy where I was. I couldn't see how I could possibly be happier anywhere else. *If they say we're definitely going, then I could run away*, I thought. *Then they would have to stay*. But where would I run away to? I could go to Darren's, but they'd soon find me there. I felt like a rat caught in a trap. There was nothing I could do.

"If you move to Canada," Darren said suddenly, "I could come and visit you in the holidays."

"It's too far," I said.

"I could come for the summer holidays," Darren said. "Although, I suppose that would be the winter over there, wouldn't it?"

"I don't know," I said. "And I don't really care."

"We could play ice hockey," Darren continued, nodding at my new shirt enthusiastically.

"I don't want to play ice hockey, Darren," I said, losing my temper. "I don't want to play any stupid Canadian game. I don't want to go to Canada. Can't you get that into your thick head?"

"I was only trying to cheer you up," Darren said huffily. "If you're going to be like that, then I'll go."

"Go on then," I said.

"Right," he said. He got up and walked into the flat and a moment or two later I heard the front door slam. I felt like I was going to explode.

As I sat there scowling, a rat came scuttling across the yard from the hole in the café wall. It stopped for an instant to pick a dandelion leaf with its teeth, then, legs splayed, it clambered up the back fence. I waited until it reached the top and then I hurled the empty Coke can at it. The can clattered against the

bottom of the fence and on to the concrete
of the yard. With a quick flick of its long tail,
the rat vanished. I went inside to my room,
lay on the bed with my face in the pillow and
cried until I fell asleep.

*   *   *

I was woken by a hand, gently stroking my hair. It was Mum.

"Hey, sleepyhead," she said. "Rise and shine, it's tea time."

If I'd been more awake I might have said I was too tired to get up. Mum was already out of the room, though, by the time my mind had really woken up. So, after a few minutes, I got slowly out of bed and trudged downstairs.

Mum had baked a delicious lemon cake for tea. It was Dad's favourite. But he only had one slice today. He looked very tired.

"Oh dear," he said, after a particularly big yawn. "It doesn't matter how often you travel, jet lag always gets you." I thought maybe he was going to be too sleepy to talk about Canada. But then, after his third cup of tea, he sat right back in his chair, sighed, looked straight at me and said, "Well, Jake..."

And I knew the moment I'd been dreading had finally arrived.

Magic

I could sense Mum and Dad staring at me
from either end of the table as I looked at the
few crumbs of lemon cake on my plate and
wondered what to say. Dad had just told me
about his job offer, the house in Toronto, the
people... He'd sold Canada better than any
brochure or TV ad. He'd sounded so
enthusiastic that I felt I couldn't just say no, I
definitely didn't want to go. He would be so
disappointed and so would Mum. But this
might be my only chance to say what I really
felt. I just didn't know quite how to say it. I
raised my eyes from my plate and looked
pleadingly, first at Mum, then at Dad.

"Don't be afraid to say what you feel, Jake," Dad said. I took a deep breath.

"Well, Dad," I began, "I think Canada sounds very nice and I *would* like to stay in one place..." I hesitated.

"Yes?" Dad prompted. I thought about Miss Barnes' story and how Cleopatra had helped Ra when he was in trouble.

Help me, Cleopatra, I said to myself. *Help me to say the right thing.* And then, suddenly, the words came.

"I like it *here*, Dad," I said. "I like this house and the yard and the café. And I like school – and Darren and Puss and Miss Barnes..."

"And the rats?" Dad queried.

"I don't mind the rats," I said. "You just have to get used to them."

"Speak for yourself," Mum said. "I never want to see another rat in my life."

"They're not so bad, Mum," I said, "really."

"You *do* want to stay, don't you?" Dad said.

I nodded.

"I see," he said. "I see." He poured himself another cup of tea, looking very thoughtful.

"Well, Jake," he said, after what seemed like ages, "you'll be interested to hear that your mum feels exactly the same way you do. Not about the rats, of course – but about moving to Canada." I looked at Mum in amazement. I'd thought she was all for going.

"So," Dad said, "you'll be pleased to know I've decided to turn down the job. I've been offered something else in London anyway, so Mum and I thought we'd settle down round here somewhere – if that's OK with you. Mum says there's a nice place near the park that might suit us." He took a sip of tea. I stared at him, unable to speak.

"Well," he said. "Cheer up. I thought you'd be pleased."

"I am," I said. "I am. It's great. Thanks, Dad." I suddenly felt so relieved, so happy.

"I must tell Darren," I said.

"Better let your cat in first," Dad said. I

looked past him and saw Puss scratching at the window. I got up to let her in.

"And while we're on the subject of that cat..." Dad said. I froze, suddenly all tensed up again. Was Dad going to say I couldn't keep her?

"...You do realize, don't you, that Puss is going to have kittens?"

The next couple of months just seemed to fly by. Having Dad home was great and it made Mum much happier too. She took me along to see the house by the park one day and I had to admit it would be great to live there, even though I'd be a bit sad to leave our flat. The house was quite big inside, but there was one small bedroom up in the attic that Mum said could be mine. She called it "Jake's nest". There wasn't much of a garden, but right opposite was the park – I'd have a fantastic view of it from my bedroom window. The best thing of all, though, was that it wasn't far from where we were living now, so I'd still be able to go to see Miss Barnes regularly (Cleopatra too of course!) and go to the same school.

Every day, as Puss got fatter, I waited impatiently for the kittens to come and wondered how many there would be. Dad said she looked big enough to have about ten in her, but Darren said the usual number was three or four. He said she'd probably make a nest somewhere to have them. I tried to tempt her by leaving cupboard doors open and putting bits of rag inside to make it cosy for her – but although she'd go in and look around, she never settled. I started to get worried that maybe she would go off somewhere else, like Harry's tyre place, to have her kittens – and then I might not even see them. But it didn't happen like that.

I was brushing my teeth in the bathroom one evening when Puss came along and started making this strange sort of yelping noise. She looked right at me, then she walked to the door and looked at me again, as though she wanted me to follow her. So I did. I followed her along the corridor and into my bedroom. She jumped on the bed and got under the top bed-cover – and that's where she had her kittens! First there was a black one, then a black and white one, and then, about half an hour later, there was a ginger one – three lovely, tiny kittens...

*   *   *

I gave Darren the ginger kitten. He was delighted.

"It's the best pet I've ever had," he said.

"I hope it'll last longer than the others," I said. Miss Barnes had the other two kittens.

"They'll keep me company when you've gone," she said. "Although I don't know what Cleopatra will make of them." She looked at the green cat and I told her how I'd wished on it that we wouldn't go to Canada – and how the wish had come true.

"I think Cleopatra's magic," I said.

"Well, you may be right," said Miss Barnes. "But wishes don't just come true on their own you know, Jake. You have to make your own magic in this life." I thought about that for a moment.

"Do you mean like telling Dad I didn't want to go to Canada?" I said. Miss Barnes didn't say anything. She just looked at me with her special smile.

The day before we moved, Mum took me round to see Harry the tyre man to ask if he

minded me taking Puss away. After all, she
said, Puss did belong to him officially.

"What if he says he does mind?" I said.

"Well, at least we'll have asked," she said.
"Don't worry, Jake, no one's going to take
Puss away from you." But Harry didn't mind.

"Got more cats than I need now anyway,"
he said, "since they got rid of the rats. You
can take a couple more if you like."

"No, thanks," Mum said. "One's quite enough." I couldn't have agreed more. I had my cat now and she was all I'd ever really wanted. She was my wish come true. My very first and only pet – Jake's cat. And now she had a proper name too – a name fitting for such a special, wonderful cat. She was Puss no longer: from now on she was going to be called "Magic" – because that's exactly what she was!